ADVENTURE IN THE SNOWS

Manmohan Singh Bawa is a trekker, mountaineer and story-writer. He spends half the year in Dalhousie and the other half in Delhi.

Adventure in the Snows

Manmohan Singh Bawa

GUL MOHAR

GUL MOHAR
an Imprint of Orient Longman Private Limited

ORIENT LONGMAN PRIVATE LIMITED

Registered Office
3-6-752 Himayatnagar, Hyderabad 500 029 (A.P.), India
e-mail: *cogeneral@orientlongman.com*

Other Offices
Bangalore / Bhopal / Bhubaneshwar / Chennai
Ernakulam / Guwahati / Hyderabad / Jaipur / Kolkata
Lucknow / Mumbai / New Delhi / Patna

First published 1997
Reprinted 2002, 2007

ISBN-13: 978 81 250 1018 0
ISBN-10: 81 250 1018 1

Typeset at
OSDATA, Hyderabad 500 029

Printed at
Orion Printers Private Limited
Hyderabad 500 004

Published by
Orient Longman Private Limited
3-6-752 Himayatnagar,
Hyderabad 500 029 (A.P.), India
e-mail: *hydgeneral@orientlongman.com*

CONTENTS

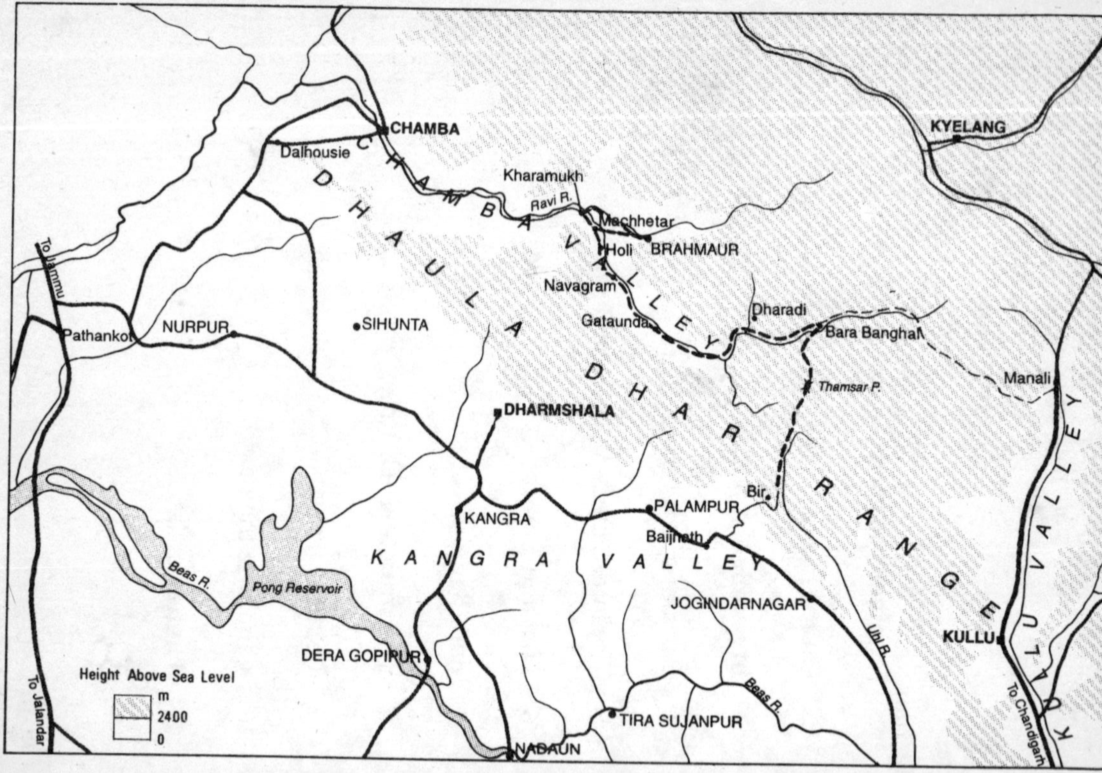

CHAMBA
KYELANG
Dalhousie
Kharamukh
Ravi R.
Machhetar
Holi
BRAHMAUR
Navagram
Gataunda
Dharadi
Bara Banghal
Manali
Thamsar P.
CHAMBA VALLEY
DHAULA DHAR RANGE
To Jammu
Pathankot
NURPUR
SIHUNTA
DHARMSHALA
Bir
PALAMPUR
Baijnath
KANGRA
KANGRA VALLEY
JOGINDARNAGAR
Uhl R.
KULLU
KULLU VALLEY
To Chandigarh
Beas R.
Pong Reservoir
DERA GOPIPUR
TIRA SUJANPUR
NADAUN
To Jalandar
Height Above Sea Level
m
2400
0

Summer Vacation

This was the second time that Pawan and Naveen had come to the beautiful hill station of Dalhousie. They had spent their last summer vacation here with their Uncle Manjit, who was a forest officer. He had a beautiful bungalow on Bakrota Hill.

Every day they would roam about on the narrow mountain tracks, collect multicoloured pebbles from the stream and look for hidden caves where black bears were said to make their home. The whole mountain-side was their playground.

On the winding mountain paths they would sometimes see woodcutters with loads of wood on their head, the coal sellers, the Gujjar milkmaids, and the legendary Gaddi shepherds with their flock of sheep coming down from the high mountains.

In the evening they would climb the mountain paths and enjoy the view from the top. From here, they could clearly see the snow-capped mountain peaks, the deep valley of Chamba and the river Ravi flowing through it. And looking at the peaks and the river, many questions would arise in their minds: How far were these mountain peaks and how high would they be? Where did the river Ravi come from?

Often Pawan would pester his elder brother Naveen with these questions. He pestered every other person who came to meet Uncle. His best friend was a Gujjar, Lachhu Singh, who had a baggage of stories.

One of Lachhu's favourite stories was about how he lost his buffalo and went looking for the creature in the jungle on the mountain slopes. Finding her sitting under a tree, Lachhu Singh shouted at her, "You unfaithful animal. How dare you make me run around the hill like a mad dog. Wait, I will give you such beating that you will not forget it for the rest of your life." Startled by his voice, the animal lumbered to its feet, and to his horror, it was not his buffalo but a huge black bear. "You won't believe how I ran for my life, *Chhote Sahib,* as if ten demonesses were after me. I ran downhill all the way because bears can't see very well while running downhill. Their long hair cover their eyes and block their vision . . ." He would narrate the story with much groaning and rolling of his eyes, while Naveen would howl with laughter.

One evening as they stood absorbed looking at the unending mountain ranges, they saw a Gaddi shepherd, accompanied by his son and flock of sheep, coming down. The two unloaded the burden they were carrying on their backs and it seemed that they were preparing to camp at that spot for the night.

Hesitatingly, Pawan and Naveen went near them. They were curious and wanted to befriend the young boy.

As they approached him, Naveen asked, "Where are you going with your sheep?"

"We are going beyond those mountains."

"Where do you live?"

"We live in the open."

"But you must have a home somewhere?"

"Yes, we have our home far beyond, beneath the snow peaks."

Pawan and Naveen looked at him with great admiration. There was so much in this world to see, to admire and to explore besides their own city and school!

When they reached home, it was already dark. Their parents and uncle were sitting on the lawn drinking tea.

"Where were you all this time? You should have returned before sunset," their mother chided them.

"Mummy, we met a shepherd boy on Bakrota hill," Pawan said excitedly.

"What is so exciting about that?" his mother asked.

"We were talking to them. They are very interesting people."

"Yes, they are," said Uncle Manjit in agreement.

"Where do they live?" Naveen asked.

"They live where the rivers have their beginning; where mountain goats, black bears, and white leopards have their home," Uncle Manjit replied.

"And where do they get food and clothes from?" Naveen asked.

"They are self-supporting people and do not depend upon cities for their daily needs. Their lifestyles have changed little from what it was thousands of years ago," Uncle Manjit explained.

The children found all this information very interesting. "And where does this river Ravi begin?" Naveen enquired.

"Its source is a glacier near a village called Bara Banghal."

"Glacier! What is a glacier?" asked Naveen.

"And where is this glacier?" Pawan wanted to know.

"One at a time," Uncle Manjit said smiling. "Have you not seen a glacier? It is a slow-moving river of hard ice. This glacier is situated just below those high peaks which you see from Bakrota hill."

At night, Pawan and Naveen could not sleep. They wanted to venture into the unknown, to encounter the dizzy heights of snow-capped peaks, visit the tiny hamlets where the Gaddi people live, and see the meadows and the glaciers from where the mighty rivers flow.

They also knew that Uncle Manjit was a carefree and adventurous man—he had gone trekking deep into the unknown beyond these mountains many a time, crossing high passes, and had even climbed snow-covered peaks.

Next morning, they tried to persuade their uncle to take them to the source of Ravi and to the land of the Gaddi shepherds. But Uncle Manjit would not agree. "The mountain paths are very difficult and hazardous. You will get tired. You will have to walk for days on end and carry your own load on your back."

"We are not afraid of hardships," said Pawan.

"I appreciate your spirit of adventure, but you don't know what is in store. Often there are no paths, which have probably been washed down by rains or lost in a landslide. You will have to negotiate rocky walls, pitch your own tents and cook your own food," Uncle gently pointed out.

"But one has got to make a start somewhere someday," Naveen said.

"Yes, that is true," Uncle Manjit agreed, adding, "then we shall do the initial training in and around Dalhousie. When you gain confidence and are fit, I shall take you to the high mountains."

Their mother could not imagine her sons roughing it out and refused to let the boys out of her sight. After much tears and persuasion, she reluctantly gave permission.

* * *

For five days they practised walking on the narrow mountain paths carrying heavy haversacks on their backs. In the beginning, they used to tire quickly, and complain. But after three or four days they got used to walking long distances. They also received some basic lessons in rock climbing from their uncle. He showed them how to find hand-holds and foot-holds in the rocks. It was great fun, and when they returned home, they were full of mountain talk. Even their appetites were enormous.

On the last day of the practice, Uncle Manjit told them that they would go for a real long walk.

"Where shall we go?" asked Naveen.

"We shall go through the Kala Top Wildlife Sanctuary," answered Uncle Manjit.

"What is a sanctuary?" Pawan wanted to know.

"A sanctuary is where wild animals are not allowed to be shot or killed by anyone, you ignoramus," replied Naveen with a know-it-all smile.

"What kind of animals live there?" asked Pawan.

"Bear, leopard, mountain goat, fox, marmot, etc.," said Uncle.

"Won't they attack us?" enquired Pawan.

"Shall we be able to see them?" asked Naveen.

"These animals are in fact very gentle. They do not attack until they are attacked by man. And we may or may not see any of them. They are very shy of men. But I have seen bears and mountain goats in this jungle several times," explained Uncle Manjit.

"You will be the first one to run away when a leopard or bear appears before you," Pawan teased Naveen.

"It won't be me, but you," Naveen retorted.

They walked up to the edge of the forest with Uncle Manjit. A signboard on a deodar tree said, 'Kala Top Wildlife Sanctuary. Disturbing and shooting animals and birds strictly prohibited'. Beneath the tree sat a swarthy man smoking a *bidi*. He looked at them suspiciously, stood up with faltering steps, and said,

"Can't you see this signboard? Men are not allowed to enter this forest."

"Who are you to question us?" Uncle asked boldly.

"I . . . I am a forest guard," answered the man.

Uncle Manjit knew all the forest guards personally and had seen the guard of this area going towards Dalhousie town. He looked at the man suspiciously and said, "You are telling a lie. I saw the guard going to the town this very morning."

The man was taken aback. He said, "Whoever I am, I am saying this for your benefit. A huge bear has been spotted in the forest. Just yesterday tore it off a man's face. You wouldn't like to see the pretty faces of these young children mangled by that bear, would you?"

There were signs of fear on Pawan and Naveen's faces.

"Don't get afraid of his wild talk. He is telling a lie. Bears generally come out of their hideout during the night. It must be sleeping peacefully in its cave somewhere," Uncle Manjit reassured them.

As they left the man behind and started walking on the narrow forest path, Uncle Manjit wondered, why that man was trying to stop them? "There seems to be something fishy going on," he said to himself.

They followed the narrow path for a while. They had hardly walked for about an hour in the forest when they heard a gunshot not very far from them. All the three stood still. Pawan and Naveen looked at Uncle with questioning eyes. Uncle Manjit looked around and then said, "I had some inkling of this when I saw that man at the edge of the forest. Some poachers are shooting the animals. They might have shot a wild goat or deer. Let's go and find out."

Uncle made a guess as to the direction from which the gunshot had come, and then led Pawan and Naveen up a slippery slope. After walking for some time, they suddenly reached a grassy opening. Two villagers were seen seated on their haunches. One of them was holding an old-fashioned gun in his right hand.

The two men were surprised to see the trekkers. They stood up and looked at them menacingly, trying to outstare them. Uncle Manjit stared back boldly and said in a booming voice, "What are you doing here with a gun? Don't you know that shooting or hunting is illegal in this forest?"

"There is only one law in the jungle," replied the man with the gun. "The law of the gun." It was evident that they had not recognised the forest officer.

Uncle Manjit retorted angrily, "You will know the law when you go to jail."

"We are the Rajasahib's men. Nobody can touch us," replied the second man arrogantly.

"The Raja is not beyond the law," said Uncle Manjit.

The man with the gun looked at him scornfully and said, "The law is only for the poor. I have seen Raja-sahib hunting leopard in this forest in the company of big officers. Go and see the leopard's skin hanging on the wall of his drawing room and take action if you dare."

Uncle listened to his plain, rough talk, pondered for a while and said, "It seems that you are telling the truth."

The man with the gun looked at the three of them and said softly, "Please sit down, *Babuji*, and let these children take some rest. They must be tired."

They sat down on the grass. Uncle said, "What I want to say is that it is wrong to kill these harmless animals."

"We are not shooting them for the fun of it, Sir. The Rajasahib ordered us to kill a deer to prepare dinner for his important city guests. But we have not killed any deer, yet."

"We understand what you are saying," replied the other man. "Anyhow these children must be feeling hungry. It is almost lunchtime. We have a few gram *chapatis* and some pickle. The water in the spring nearby is very cool and refreshing . . . ." Saying this, he took out a bundle from his bag. Soon they were talking, laughing and eating like old friends.

* * *

Pawan and Naveen waited restlessly for the adventure to begin. But a few preliminaries still had to be attended to. They had to chalk out the route.

Spreading a map on the table, Uncle Manjit explained to Pawan and Naveen, "We shall follow the river Ravi up to Bara Banghal and from there we shall cross one of the snow-covered mountain passes and reach Kulu or Kangra Valley."

"It does not seem difficult," Pawan observed. "We shall be walking along the banks of the Ravi to reach Bara Banghal, isn't it?"

"Yes, it looks very simple on the map. But you will know the facts only when you actually tread these paths."

As they had to spend two weeks amidst the mountains and carry the load themselves, they made their list of requirements very carefully. Every essential item should be included, but they should not overload their bags. They purchased the necessary provisions and collected the following equipment: a light-weight tent, rucksacks, haversacks, sleeping bags, kerosene, a stove, a pressure cooker and utensils, lantern and candles torches, pocket-knives, an axe, a compass, sunglasses, hunter-shoes, pullovers, wind-proof jackets, woollen socks, needle and thread, a first-aid kit, etc.

Luckily, they were able to get some of the equipment from Dalhousie itself. Many foreign tourists and trekkers come to this hill station and, when leaving, sell their equipment to Tibetan refugees. The latter, in turn, sell these things along with their traditional wares such as sweaters and shawls.

The route was considered in detail. It was decided that they would go to Chamba which was fifty-two kilometres by bus, spend a day or two there, then take another bus for Kharamukh. From Kharamukh they would start their journey on foot. Walking along the river Ravi, they would reach the last village, Bara Banghal. From there, they would cross one of the high passes to reach either the Kulu or Kangra valleys, depending on the snow and weather conditions.

On the move

They packed everything into their rucksacks and reached Chamba by bus the next morning. Chamba is situated on the banks of the Ravi and is a small, pretty hill town. They stayed there for a day, saw the ancient temples, and the next day boarded the bus for Kharamukh.

For the first one hour, the bus went along the banks of the Ravi and then crossed the river over a bridge to the right side. The road now became very narrow. On one side, was the gushing waters of the river and on the other, the rocky wall of the mountain. At every bend, it seemed as if the bus would fall into the river. The driver was efficient and they heaved a sigh of relief as they reached Kharamukh safely.

They unloaded their luggage from the bus and sat down on a rough bench in front of a tea-shop. "It will help if we could have a wholesome breakfast before we start on foot," Uncle Manjit suggested.

Many people were seen eating fried grams and *pakoras*. They too ordered the same.

After breakfast Pawan wanted to know which way they would go.

"We shall cross the Ravi over the bridge and then follow the Budhal Nala," Uncle Manjit told them.

Pawan and Naveen's faces turned white as they looked at the chasm below the rope bridge. But they picked up their rucksacks and stood up.

"Let's go," Uncle Manjit said. There was a new vigour in his voice.

Pawan and Naveen adjusted their rucksacks on their backs and stepped forward. It was their first step towards the unseen, unknown paths, the dizzy heights, the emerald-coloured highland lakes and the snow-capped summits.

They smiled as they looked at each other. They imagined themselves to be great mountaineers and adventurers, whose photographs they had seen in the newspapers. Explorers who had climbed high peaks, gone to the North and South Poles, discovered new continents and found their way through the dense forests of Africa and South America. Though they carried heavy loads on their backs, their hearts were light.

With their hearts in their mouths, they crossed the river over the rope bridge, which swung as they walked. The river water gushed and roared down below. They reached the other side and started walking along the Budhal Nala. The road on which they were walking cut through the rocky mountain. The rocks hanging over their heads provided shelter from sun and rain. Far below, Budhal Nala had chiselled its way through the mountain, forming a deep gorge. The river looked like a white ribbon in the distance.

After walking for about twelve kilometres, they took a sharp turn and beheld a wonderful spectacle which held them spellbound. Before them stood a small town which was situated on a gentle slope. The golden *kalash* (domes) of the temples were shining bright in the centre of the town, which was surrounded by snow-covered mountains, giving it the shape of a huge snow cup. Giant pine trees stood majestically on the hilly slopes. White sheep grazed silently on the green meadows.

* * *

They had come to the ancient town of Brahmaur. On arriving, the group was told that the dak bungalow was occupied by some government officials.

"What should we do now?" Pawan looked worried.

"We shall find some other place or can pitch our tents somewhere," Uncle Manjit assured him.

As they approached the town, they noticed two young men standing on the road. From their dress they looked like outsiders. When they came nearer, one of the young men wished them good afternoon and asked, how they happened to come to this godforsaken place.

Uncle Manjit explained their plan to them and enquired if a place to stay could be found.

"In case you have no objection you are welcome to stay with us," the men offered.

"But you do not seem to belong to this place," Uncle said.

"You are right," they replied. "We are students of anthropology and have come here to study the social customs and way of life of the Gaddi people."

They accompanied the young men to their home and after resting awhile went to see the temples of Brahmaur situated in a place called Chaurasi*.

Wandering around Chaurasi, they saw many Gaddi men sitting on the temple platforms, puffing their *hukka* and gossiping. They were wearing white woollen *cholas* and their legs were bare. The *cholas* were gathered round the waist by a long black cord.

"Why do they tie this cord round their waist?" Pawan asked the anthropology students.

"It keeps their stomachs warm and gives their long dress some shape," they told him.

They saw some women wearing long *cholas*, gracefully carrying brass pitchers on their heads, filled

---

***Chaurasi* means eighty-four, taking its name from the eighty-four temples found there.

with water from a spring nearby. Around their waist too was tied the woollen cord.

They learnt that the Gaddi are extremely simple, healthy and strong people. Theft or any other type of crime is rare among them. The women, called Gaddans, are one of the prettiest and healthiest women in India. "The Gaddi are believed to be of pure Aryan origin," the students told them. "They came to India about three-thousand years ago and settled in the cool and grassy slopes of Dhauladhar."

"Tell me more about them," Naveen pleaded.

"You are going to pass through their village and you will see everything for yourself," the students replied.

*   *   *

At Brahmaur they bought the necessary provisions and bid goodbye to their hosts. They were told that there would be no shops *en route* for many days to come. Now their loads became very heavy and they had to engage a porter.

Their next destination was a village called Holi. They climbed a ridge and then descended. After a four-hour trek they crossed the Ravi again and reached a place called Machhetar. A European and an Indian youth were having tea in a shop. They looked familiar; Pawan and Naveen had seen them in Dalhousie.

"Where are you headed for?" the European asked them.

"We are going towards Bara Banghal," Uncle Manjit replied.

"And from Bara Banghal which pass do you intend to cross?" the Indian asked.

"It depends on the weather and the circumstances. We may cross the Kaliheni Pass or any of the other passes," Uncle replied.

"We are also headed in the same direction. Can we join you?" they asked.

"The more the merrier," Uncle responded enthusiastically.

They introduced themselves. David was from Canada and Bhushan had come from Delhi. David was a botanist and could distinguish between edible and inedible wild plants. This knowledge was to come in handy later on when they lost their way and their provisions ran out.

After biscuits and tea, the group of five picked up their rucksacks and started on their long trek.

"Five is a lucky number," Bhushan observed.

"Well, yes," Uncle agreed with a smile.

They made an early halt on that day and rested in a big natural cave near the bank of a stream. All five of them could fit in easily. The following day, they reached Holi. The porter who was accompanying them left them in Holi and went back.

IN SEARCH OF A PORTER

The party pitched tents near a spring on the outskirts of the village. Uncle, Bhushan and Naveen went into the village in search of a porter. Soon they were surrounded by curious Gaddi folk and their bright-eyed children. They asked if someone from the village was willing to accompany them as a porter-cum-guide. They were willing to pay them.

"What shall we do with money when we can get everything we need without it?" One of them said in jest at the offer.

"No one from this village has ever crossed over to that side. The track is very dangerous," another observed.

"But why are you going there? Take some easier route," a third villager suggested.

They returned to the camp disappointed. It was impossible for them to walk on these unknown paths alone with the load of tents, utensils and rations on their backs.

Someone had told them that they might get porters from another village which was situated atop the hill.

"All right," Uncle said, "tomorrow we shall try our luck there. Now that we have come so far, we are not going back. We will find some way out, or God may send someone . . ."

As they were sitting around the fire after dinner, a tall, well-built Gaddi came to them and sat down beside them, greeting them with a *Jai Hind*. He looked at them for some time and said, "I have heard that you are planning to go to Bara Banghal?"

"We are not just planning to, we are going," Uncle Manjit replied.

"Along with these children?" he looked surprised. "Even we seldom go that way."

"Yes, why not? Your people also cross these mountains with your children," Uncle was quick to respond.

"Our case is different. We are born and brought up amidst these rough mountains. Our hands and feet are like rocks and our legs like that of the ibex."

"Then let them also grow strong," Uncle said, looking at Pawan and Naveen proudly. "Let their feet get blisters, let their legs become swollen; only then will they become strong and tough like you."

"Well said," the Gaddi applauded.

Uncle Manjit and Bhushan admired this illiterate Gaddi's confidence. He was aware of things which mattered. Uncle looked at him and queried, "So when should we start?"

"How can you be so sure?" the Gaddi enquired.

"Because I know you will go. You are fearless and selfless."

"We will start tomorrow morning. My village is on the way. You can stay in my village for one day while I go and fetch my clothing and equipment from the grazing ground. My sheep are up there on the mountain slopes," he said pointing upwards.

"What is your name?" Bhushan asked.

"Sansar Chand," he replied.

"How much will you charge?"

"I am not going with you for money. I am going because no outsider has ever been there and I admire your guts," he replied. "And one more thing, I shall go with you for three stages only, up to the village Dharadi."

After that he got up and disappeared into the dark. There was complete silence except for the murmuring of a stream nearby. The sky was clear and the stars seemed to be within reach. The trekkers were filled with peace and happiness.

* * *

Sansar Chand come back early the next morning. They packed up everything and reached his village. There they bathed and washed their clothes. They knew that they wouldn't have such an opportunity later during their trek.

Then they went around the village. They observed that the houses were made of wood and were usually double storied. The ground floor was used for cattle and fodder and the first floor for living purposes.

Naveen saw something in the verandah and asked, "What is that?"

"That is their loom. They weave their blankets and clothes with their own hands," Uncle said, pointing to a wooden beam machine. He added that they got wool from sheep and had their own cows and goats, which provided them with milk, ghee and hide. The Gaddi also had their own fields where they sowed wheat, barley, pulses and other crops.

There were more women than men in that village. Most of the men had gone to the distant mountain ranges with their flocks of sheep, while a few were preparing to leave. Sansar Chand told them that he too would be leaving with his sheep soon because there weren't enough pastures on the surrounding slopes. Hence he could not accompany them for more than three stages of the trek.

* * *

While they were exploring the village, they heard the cries of a dog. They hurried to the spot to see a big, black, shaggy dog tied to a tree. A man was beating him mercilessly with a stick.

Naveen sprang forward and cried, "Don't hit the poor creature. Have you no mercy."

The angry man spat back, "It 's my dog. I will do whatever I want with it. The wretched animal is a thief, he steal hens, chases and bites people."

Uncle Manjit was very fond of dogs and could immediately recognise the traits of each breed. He looked at the dog carefully and enquired, "Will you sell him to me?"

"You can have this ill-tempered thief for no price. I shall only be too happy to get rid of this rascal," the villager scowled and said.

"All right, then do one thing. Bring this dog to my camp and tie him to a tree. I will handle the rest," Uncle said.

Uncle purchased a kilo of goat's meat and went to the campsite. The dog had already been tied to a tree. He saw Uncle and snarled at him furiously. Uncle took a piece of meat and stepped cautiously towards the angry dog. He gazed into the dog's eyes, and whispering softly to him, threw him a piece of meat.

The dog started to eat greedily. Uncle gave him some more. When the dog had finished most of it, Uncle went near him, patted his head, caressed him and untied him from the tree. He again whispered something in his ear and led him into the nearby forest.

After an hour, when they returned, Pawan and Naveen observed to their astonishment that the dog had become very tame and docile. They named him Tiger, and were happy to have this addition to their group.

* * *

Early next morning Sansar Chand arrived carrying his woollen blanket, axe and the other items necessary for the journey. They divided the load according to the capacity of each trekker and started off. For the first few hours they walked on level ground. After that the path started climbing. As they proceeded, the path became steeper and steeper.

They walked on these uneven paths for two days, ascending and descending, crossing streams, passing through small villages and thick forests. On the third day, as they climbed a steep ridge, they discovered that the track on which they had been walking had disappeared completely. Ahead was a steep, rocky wall, about two hundred metres wide, making an angle of seventy degrees. It ended in the river Ravi, which was three-hundred metres below.

"Which side are we to go now?" Naveen asked.

"We have to traverse this rocky wall," Sansar Chand said.

Pawan and Naveen could not believe their ears. How were they to climb? There was no path; there were no holds even for their small feet!

"How can we do it? We will just slide down into the river!" they exclaimed.

Sansar Chand allayed their fears saying, "There are small cracks and ledges. These are not visible from a distance. Just see how I do it."

Then, to their amazement, with the agility of a goat, he started crossing the rocky wall. His feet found small ledges and his hands gripped hand-holds. After giving them this demonstration, he came back.

"But if someone slips?" Pawan asked. He was nervous.

"He will fall straight into the river," Sansar Chand said lightly.

"But we shall not take unnecessary risks," Uncle Manjit said. "We shall cross this portion with the help of a rope."

"That's right," David agreed quickly, quite relieved.

Uncle Manjit took a long rope out of his rucksack. Bhushan volunteered to go first. He tied one end of the rope to his waist. Finding his way up with the help of ledges and cracks, he crossed carefully. Soon, he reached safe and ground level. He untied the rope from his waist, tied it to a protruding rock and then asked David to cross with the help of the rope. David first looked at the rope and then towards the river down below and felt nervous. Understanding his hesitation, Bhushan said encouragingly, "Don't look below and don't be afraid; it is not difficult."

"But if something happens? If my foot slips?"

"Nothing will happen. Just concentrate on the rope and on your feet."

"No," David said firmly. "Though I do not have a family and my parents won't miss me much, I do not want to die so soon and so far away from home."

Bhushan wanted to laugh, but Uncle told him in Hindi not to. Then addressing David he said, "Unnecessary fear and carelessness are two things that are dangerous in the mountains. Since we have taken all precautions there is nothing to fear. Then, just to give him confidence, Uncle took hold of the rope and, stepping on the ledges of the rocks, crossed it.

When David saw the ease with which Uncle Manjit came back, he gathered courage. He took hold of the rope and stepped forward. After the first two steps, his self-confidence was restored and he crossed the rock wall. As he took the last step and stood near

Bhushan on the broad ledge, a smile of satisfaction and accomplishment spread on his face. He pushed back his hair which had partly covered his eyes, and uttered, "So I have done it at last!"

It was Pawan's turn now. He put on a brave face, held the rope tight in his hand and started climbing, stepping on the ledges and cracks of the rock wall. After a few steps, as he looked down, one-thousand feet below, an unknown fear gripped his mind. Suddenly his left foot slipped, his knee hit a rock and a cry of fear escaped his throat.

"Hold on," cried Uncle Manjit, "I am coming." With that, he started shooting instructions, "David, you hold on to the other end of the rope tightly." Soothing Pawan, he said in a calm voice, "Keep a tight grip on the rope and pull your leg up slowly." Saying this, he inched along the rock wall trying to reach Pawan. On reaching him, he held his arm firmly in his right hand and pulled him up. This done, Pawan managed to find a ledge again and after a pause inched his way up slowly on shaky feet.

"Well done," exclaimed Uncle and Bhushan together as he reached the other end.

Naveen, gaining from the experience of David and Pawan, was able to cross the rock wall slowly and carefully.

The only one who did not use the rope, and in fact seemed amused at this exercise, was Tiger. He was able to cross the gorge like a goat. Perhaps he was accustomed to it.

After that they descended a slope and reached the bank of a gushing stream. Pawan and Naveen noticed that whenever they climbed one side of a mountain, they invariably had to descend down to a stream or a river. And after crossing the stream, they would again find themselves climbing up.

Very tired of the exercise, Naveen exclaimed, "Uncle, what is the use of climbing up if we have to come down? Is there no easy and even path?"

Uncle Manjit looked at him smilingly and said, "Mountains are like life, full of ups and downs."

The stream was coming down from the high mountains with fearful rapidity. There was a narrow log bridge over it. The bridge was balanced precariously on both sides on rocks. It was so flimsy that it started swinging with the load of single person. The party crossed it carefully, one by one.

They were tired and hungry by this time so they prepared lunch. As they were stretching their tired limbs after the meal, they saw grey clouds covering the sky.

"I am afraid we shall have to move immediately. It can start raining any time," Sansar Chand declared.

"I am dead tired and cannot walk a single step more," Pawan protested.

"Can't we pitch our tents here? It is such a nice spot and there is water nearby," Naveen added.

"No, we can't camp here. We are on a slope and if it rains, which I am sure it will, our tents would be washed away," Uncle Manjit said.

"Then where shall we halt today?" Pawan asked.

"There is a village on top of the hill," Sansar Chand said pointing up. "I have some relatives there. We can stay with them."

"On the top of the hill?" Pawan cried. "Oh my God! Another climb? I am simply sick of this climbing."

"The village cannot come down. You will have to climb to the village," Uncle Manjit said laughing.

"How far is it from here?"

"The distance is not much but it is very steep."

There was no other way than to get up and start walking.

"Give me your rucksack," Bhushan tried to help Pawan, who was the youngest. Pawan declined the offer though he would have loved to be rid of his load. Uncle Manjit gave him a pat on the back and said encouragingly, "All right then, let us go."

They climbed and climbed the narrow, rocky, steep path. They kept on walking till they could walk no more and rested only to start again. Sounds of distant thunder filled the skies. The air became very cold. While they could feel the cold on their faces and hands, they were warm inside, warm with the toil of the day, with the labour of climbing.

And then small flakes of snow fell. It was beautiful, but the boys were not in a mood to appreciate. They wanted to reach their destination as soon as possible. Now they were walking on a higher altitude and experienced some difficulty in breathing. They had to stop to rest after every few minutes.

PARTAKING IN A CEREMONY

What a relief it was to reach level ground. From here they could see the houses of the village Dharadi. The slated roofs were covered with snow. The smoke which swirled from the chimneys was soon diffused and dispersed by the cold air.

They reached the house which Sansar Chand had mentioned earlier and dropped their load in the verandah. The lady of the house peeped out. A look of surprise spread on her face as she saw this small group of people standing outside. She invited them into the warmth of her house.

It had become freezingly cold by now and their toes were getting numb. A fire was burning in a corner of the room. The dim light of the fire fell on the windowless walls. They saw necklace-like black shapes hanging from the roof, formed due to the smoke inside the room. As they sat around the fire the warmth soothed them.

"Where are you coming from?" the woman asked.

"Delhi," Bhushan replied.

"Is it as big a place as Chamba?" she asked.

"Much bigger."

"I have heard that there are rooms on wheels which run on very broad paths there?"

"Yes, they are called cars or buses."

"And my husband tells me that he has seen *trains* which run on iron rails."

"Yes, Mother, have you never been to Delhi?" Naveen asked,

"No," she said, "tell me more about it."

They told her about electricity, the lamps which light automatically, the boxes which speak or sing, the big multi-storey buildings, rows of shops where everything is available. She listened with awe, finding it all beyond her imagination.

"Are we going to pitch our tents somewhere or are we staying here?" Pawan asked.

"You can stay in the house if you like," Sansar Chand said.

They heaved a sigh of relief. They were so tired that they had no energy left to pitch the tents. And moreover, who would like to leave the comfort of a cozy room in such weather?

Next morning, when the trekkers came out on the verandah they found many old men, women and children gathered in front of the house. The previous night, Uncle Manjit had treated the woman's son for sore eyes. Word had spread, and now all these people had come to get some medical aid for their minor ailments.

"Is there no doctor or dispensary in the village?" Pawan asked.

"There is no medical aid for miles around," an old man replied

"Then what do you do when you fall sick?"

"What can we do? We get some herbs from the jungle. Sometimes we are cured, sometimes not," the old man replied. "But God is very kind to us. It is very seldom that our people suffer from any serious illness. Our weak children die before they are a year old. Those who survive, die either of old age or in an accident."

Bhushan, Uncle Manjit and David got busy examining the villagers and distributing medicines from their first aid kit. Since the ailments were minor and elementary ones, they had no difficulty finding the right medicine.

From here, Sansar Chand was to turn back. Once again they were left without a porter. Sansar Chand promised to arrange porters before he went back. It would not be difficult since their free medical aid and friendliness had earned them a lot of goodwill amongst the villagers.

Uncle Manjit and Bhushan, accompanied by Sansar Chand, went to the headman of the village. They found him sympathetic. He called a meeting of the village people. They talked for a long time. Ultimately, a father and son agreed to go with them. The porter's load was to be divided between them because of the hazardous nature of the terrain.

They also laid down two conditions. One, that the journey was to be postponed by two days, as they had some very important ceremony in their house. The other condition was a pleasant one—they wanted the trekkers to take part in the ceremony, which Uncle Manjit and the others readily accepted.

* * *

The ceremony, called *Nawala*, was being held in the porters' newly built house. When Pawan, Naveen and their friends arrived, they saw a man called *chela* sitting cross-legged in the middle of a crowd. Incense burnt before him. After some time they observed that his body trembled and his head swung violently. Soon he went into a frenzy. The people believed that he had been possessed by Lord Shiva. Then all of a sudden he stopped swaying. This was the time to ask questions. People began to shoot all kinds of questions at him; he answered each of them promptly.

Pawan, Naveen and the others were also invited to ask questions.

"Shall we complete our journey successfully?" enquired Uncle Manjit.

The *chela* shivered and said, "I see many obstacles."

"Will we be able to overcome these obstacles?" asked Uncle.

"Yes, Yes, if you pray and make some offering in the temple of Shiva."

There was great festivity all around. The villagers were enjoying themselves. In one corner, a dozen people were playing the game of *chaupat*. It reminded Uncle Manjit of the great Pandavas and Kauravas. At another corner, the musicians, and drummers were getting ready for a performance.

Just before sunset, the young men of the village, wearing white *cholas* and white turbans, gathered in a big compound. They danced in a circle, swaying their bodies in an easy and graceful manner. The dance was accompanied by traditional folk songs. The tempo of the dance increased to the accompaniment of the *shehnai*, drum and *karna*—a long brass pipe. The dance occasionally reached a frenzy, with the dancer's white *cholas* flying and whirling around.

Their songs though long, were enchanting. One went:

I miss you terribly my Gaddi
I miss you very much;
With naked feet I climb the hill
hoping to see you return;
My feet are pierced by sharp thorns
and of you there is no sign.

Naveen memorised a part of the famous folk song *kunjua*, which went something like this:

I weep profusely
while washing clothes O Kunjua
come and speak to me, please
come and listen to me.

He sang it all through the evening till Pawan threatened to gag him.

The Forest, the Bear, and the Storm

Both the porters were lean and agile, as hillmen usually are. The father wore a white turban and carried a small *hukka* tucked safely under the coils of rope around his belly. He was about fifty-five years old. The son was twenty, and wore a white cap over his head. The former had been to Bara Banghal, but that was many years ago, so his memory of the route was vague. The route was completely new for the younger one. They had a very good reason for going with the trekkers. The old man had a sister who was married in Bara Banghal. He had not seen her for the last twenty years or more.

After the group had proceeded a little distance they realised why the villagers had been reluctant to accompany them on this trek. Sometimes the narrow track would disappear among the sea of rocks, at other times, they had to climb almost perpendicular cliffs with the help of a rope. After every few hundred metres, the track would lead down through a precipitous descent, as if they were heading towards a deep hole. Then again they would have to climb till their limbs ached, and they would rest perspiring, leaning on a boulder or a tree trunk. Sometimes they had to force their way through the dense forest amongst fallen deodar trees.

They walked the whole day till the light faded. According to their information Bara Banghal was twenty-four kilometres away from Dharadi, the village from where they had started in the morning.

"How far is Bara Banghal from here?" Bhushan asked the porters.

"I do not know exactly, but we still have a long way to go."

"Then we shall make a halt for the night at a suitable place," Uncle said.

On ascending a forest path, they reached a beautiful small lake. They heaved a sigh of relief and struck their tents for the night.

During the last few days, they had learnt to do the jobs allotted to them efficiently. David and Naveen pitched the tents; the porters brought water and collected wood. Bhushan and Uncle Manjit started preparing the meal and Pawan, helped them by doing odd jobs.

Having finished the alloted task, Naveen sat down on a big rock, a little distance away from the tents. From here he looked at the red and yellow tents. Nearby, the amber of the fire in the makeshift hearth was shining like gold. They were surrounded by a thick pine forest. The forest seemed to be murmuring. This was an old, dense, pine forest, untouched yet by saw or axe. The slanting rays of the setting sun penetrated between the tree trunks. Everything was unimaginably beautiful. Naveen's heart was filled with joy. He had never felt such ecstasy in his life before.

* * *

During their travel they had seen a pair of marmots, a few mountain goats and a pair of monals, (a pheasant). It was said that there were plenty of black bears and leopards in this area; but they had not yet encountered any of these creatures.

Their dog Tiger had been feeling uneasy ever since they struck their tents, but no one paid any special attention to him. After the meal, everyone retired to the tents, while the two Gaddi porters rekindled the fire and slept between two big boulders in the open. Tiger also preferred spending the night near the fire in the open.

At about midnight, there was a great commotion, and everyone woke up. Uncle Manjit, Pawan and Naveen came out of their tents. Their torchlight revealed Tiger blocking the path of a big black bear, barking furiously. The bear was also howling at Tiger. It seemed that they would soon pounce upon each other. The Gaddi porters took out two logs of burning wood and rushed at the bear. The bear, outnumbered and frightened, beat a hasty retreat.

Tiger came back triumphantly towards Uncle Manjit and looked at him for approval. Uncle patted

him on his back and said, "Well done, Tiger, well done!"

As they all settled down around the fire, Pawan asked, "What would have happened if Tiger was not with us?"

"Nothing much!" Uncle replied. "Perhaps the bear felt a little curious and was annoyed at our intruding into his territory. These forest animals never attack without provocation."

Pawan nodded and kept silent. The old Gaddi threw more wood into the fire. There was a sort of humming in the forest which they could just hear. A dark cloud drifted from behind the dense forest, covering the few stars in the sky. The old Gaddi raised his head and listened.

Uncle Manjit looked at him and sensed that something was wrong.

"What is it?" he asked.

"Ah, I know it, for I know what the trees are saying," the Gaddi said. "A storm is in the offing. See, the branches have started stirring. It may be a thunderstorm, or something worse, but don't get frightened. We are in a deep valley. The storm will come and pass off."

As he was talking, the wind shook the branches of the surrounding pines and the noise from the forest rose to a crescendo. In a matter of minutes, the whole sky was covered with thundering, threatening clouds. Tiger also looked around apprehensively.

"Everybody to his tent," the old Gaddi ordered.

"And you?" Uncle Manjit asked.

"We shall look for shelter in a cave."

But there was no time for them to look for a cave. It had already started raining, and Uncle Manjit dragged them into his four-men tent.

Soon the water poured down in sheets, while strong winds blew around them. David and Bhushan were in one tent. While Pawan, Naveen, Uncle Manjit, the two Gaddis and Tiger sat bundled in the other. It rained hard, throughout the night, and continued to pour even on the following day.

They prepared their breakfast over the kerosene stove in the tent and waited for the rain to stop. It was already past 11.00 a.m. when it stopped. Everyone came out of the tents and looked around. The sky was clear, but the level of the lake had risen considerably. They could also see many waterfalls which had sprung up during the night.

"Should we start now?" Bhushan asked.

"No, we should not," the old Gaddi advised. "All the streams on our route would be swollen and we would not be able to cross them because there are no bridges over them. It is advisable to stay on here for sometime."

"But we cannot afford to remain here. We do not have enough to eat and we have used up most of the rations," Uncle said.

They had been told that there were some shops in Bara Banghal where they could purchase provisions. Keeping this in mind, they had carried only enough provisions to last them for two days. They discussed the situation and decided to pack up and leave immediately in the hope that, with speed and good luck they should be able to reach Bara Banghal the same day.

Lost and Found

But luck had something else in store for them. Due to heavy rainfall and the falling of leaves, the track, which was hardly visible originally, had disappeared completely. The old Gaddi led them according to his conjecture. Soon they had to make a stop. A small tributary of the Ravi had swollen up into a big stream, barring their progress. Its waters gushed down with great force, carrying mud and stones along with it, making it impossible to ford it.

"It may be narrower at some place upstream," suggested the old Gaddi.

So they started upstream. The climb over big boulders and through wet vegetation was not an easy one. After walking for an hour, they found a suitable place and crossed the stream with the help of ropes. But no sooner had they crossed, when they found that they had lost their track and sense of direction completely.

Uncle Manjit asked everyone to unload and sit at one place. He took Bhushan and Tiger with him to look for the track. After sometime they came back and informed the group that they had seen some fresh droppings of sheep leading upwards. "Then there must be some hamlet or shepherd hut nearby," the porters observed.

The trekkers got up and now followed the sheep track. This time Tiger led them. They kept on climbing for an hour and finally reached a green meadow. A healthy young Gaddi was reclining against a big rock. A flock of sheep was grazing nearby, while a big black shepherd dog stood beside him closely watching every movement of the intruders.

Seeing them coming towards him, the black dog barked and rushed at Tiger. The shepherd shouted something in his dialect and the dog went back and stood beside him alert and watchful. The shepherd

looked much surprised to see them and asked where they were headed for?

"We are going towards Bara Banghal," the porters told him.

"But this track does not lead to Bara Banghal. It leads to Mani Mahesh instead," the shepherd said.

"Then which is the way to Bara Banghal?" the porter asked.

"You have deviated considerably from you track. You won't be able to reach there today."

"Then what should we do?" Bhushan enquired. "We do not have anything to eat."

"Take it easy my friend," the shepherd said. "Now drop your load and rest your tired minds and limbs. You can share whatever we have."

There was no other way. So they decided to camp there. While they all busied themselves in pitching the tents, David brought some wild plants. "These are very nourishing and will provide you with warmth and energy," he declared proudly.

The shepherd got up and removed some snow from a snow heap. From underneath he brought a large quantity of sheep's meat. "One of my sheep fell down from a cliff and fractured its leg. A sheep with a broken leg is no good, so I had to kill it. Now it is yours," he said, offering it to them.

"This is a nice way to preserve meat," said Pawan looking at the snow heap.

That night they made a big fire and cooked the meat over it. The wild vegetables tasted good and the meat provided a grand barbeque. The ate ravenously and listened to the Gaddi shepherd's tales of adventure. Amidst all this, Pawan and Naveen felt happy, strong and grown up.

Next morning, they thanked the shepherd for his hospitality and left. Now the trek became difficult. They climbed higher and higher up through the alpine meadows and over the landslide. Often, the narrow path hugged the very edge of the precipitous cliffs. They descended steeply, slipping, holding the branches of bushes. They took no rest and were eager to reach their destination.

Bara Banghal

They saw the roofs of Bara Banghal from above, and their hearts leapt with joy. When they entered the village, the lanterns had been lit, though it was not yet dark outside.

The prospect of having hot tea enlivened their spirits. But their hopes were shortlived. The tea-shop owner had also just arrived from Baijnath (in Kangra valley) and had nothing to offer them at that moment.

The old Gaddi and his son after dumping their load, went to the senior porter's sister's house at the other side of the village. Completely exhausted, with no energy left to light the stove or to do anything, the trekkers stretched their tired limbs and lay down in the verandah of the shop, which also served as the shopkeeper's house.

Seeing a fire burning inside the house, Bhushan asked the woman of the house whether they could boil their tea kettle on it. The lady hesitated, looked at their tired faces sympathetically and then invited them inside.

For the next two days and three nights it became their home. They cooked and prepared all their meals on that fire. When the Gaddi woman saw them preparing *chapatis* clumsily, she offered to make them.

Bara Banghal was a rather big village and besides the local population, there were labourers and forest contractors, who were busy cutting trees from the mountain slopes.

The villagers refused to help the trekkers; no help was forthcoming from even the headman of the village. When he came to know that they could not proceed further without the help of a mule or a porter, he tried to exploit them. He looked at them with cunning eyes and said, "All the passes are full of snow, hard ice and crevasses. It is impossible to cross them now."

"But what about Thamsar Pass?" asked Uncle Manjit.

"I don't know. It is too early to climb over that pass. There is so much snow there that even a mule will sink in it," answered the headman.

"But I have heard that some people have crossed over it three days ago. Can you provide us with porters to cross that pass?" enquired Uncle.

"Why should anybody risk his life?" retorted the headman. "But still I shall only be too glad to help you. I shall definitely ask someone to accompany you as a porter. But I am unsure what his charges will be."

Uncle Manjit and Bhushan were rather unhappy with the headman's answer and returned disappointed. After sometime, a lean and sickly looking man came to them and told them that he had been sent by the headman. He was ready to go with them as a porter, provided a few preconditions were met: he would charge Rs 400 per day; he would not carry more than fifteen kilos; and he would go only up to the top of the pass and no further.

"And what shall we do when we are on the pass?" Uncle Manjit asked sarcastically. "Sit down and meditate?"

"I do not know," he replied. "But if you want me to accompany you up to Bir then I will charge Rs 1500."

"Rupees one-thousand five-hundred!" Uncle Manjit exclaimed. "It is unreasonable!"

"You may think so, but the pass is too dangerous and I shall be risking my life by coming back alone. Wouldn't I?"

"Okay, we shall let you know," Uncle dismissed him for the time being.

It was clear that they were being exploited. The shopkeeper had told them in confidence that the headman was a crook, and had learnt the bad ways of city people. He also expressed his doubt that the headman and his henchmen were preventing other people from coming forward as porters. So a 'council of war' was held to discuss the situation.

"I do not like to be exploited like this, and we cannot afford so much money too," David initiated.

"Me too, nor do I like to feel helpless," said Uncle.

"But what can we do?" enquired Bhushan. "We cannot carry all the load ourselves. The climb is too stiff."

"And we do not know much about the path. We may get lost in the snow like the last time," Naveen added.

"But if the porter is willing to carry only fifteen kilos, and that too only up to the pass, then why not distribute the fifteen kilos amongst ourselves?" Bhushan suggested.

After some discussion they decided that they would not let themselves be exploited and would do without that porter. They calculated the distances and estimated that they could reach the next habitation on the other side of the pass in three days. They also discovered that they were carrying too many things which they actually did not need. By selling off the extra milk powder, sugar, tea leaves, the lantern, kerosene oil, etc., they could not only reduce their baggage but could also add to their diminishing cash reserves, since these commodities were scarce in this remote place.

When the headman came to know of their intention to sell their goods, he came to them along with his henchmen and enquired about the price of sugar, milk powder, tea leaves, etc.

"Sugar is Rs 50 and milk powder Rs 150 per kilo."

"That's expensive!" the headman exclaimed.

"If your man can ask for Rs 400 for one day's porterage then why can't we charge this price for our commodities? After all, we have also paid to get these things up to this place," Bhushan retorted.

The headman had no answer and bought the sugar, milk powder, and tea leaves at the prices they had quoted. While leaving, he whispered something to his companions, looked at the trekking party with challenging eyes and left. It appeared that they were up to some mischief.

David, Bhushan and Uncle Manjit weighed the pros and cons and decided to try again to get a porter or guide. In case they were unable to get someone, they would proceed alone.

* * *

Early next morning, they were told by a shepherd that there was a man with many mules and that he would possibly agree to go with them.

"But where can we find him?" asked Bhushan.

"He is somewhere on the slopes near the Ravi glacier. One of you will have to go there personally," was the reply.

As Bhushan was getting ready to go to look for the muleteer, Naveen asked, whether he could go with him.

"You will have to ask your uncle," replied Bhushan.

Naveen got permission to accompany Bhushan. They filled their haversacks with some food, and taking an ice axe they set off.

They followed the course of the river Ravi as directed by the shepherd. Since they were not carrying much load on their backs, they felt very light and made good progress. They walked for two or three hours but could not see any sign of either the mules or the man. The path was getting narrower and steeper.

Suddenly a suspicion rose in Bhushan's mind. 'Perhaps the shepherd was only a decoy sent by the headman to fool us, and there were no mules and no muleteer.' "We shall walk and see for one hour more and if we do not find the man, then we shall return," Bhushan told Naveen.

They started walking very fast now. The path was stony and slippery, but Bhushan did not care. There was accumulated snow in between the boulders so they must have gained a lot of height. Bhushan led while Naveen trailed behind.

He jumped from rock to rock very confidently, not realising the danger of doing so on wet rocks. Suddenly his foot slipped and Naveen saw him falling. He, disappeared from sight. Naveen's heart skipped a beat and he came hurriedly to the spot from where Bhushan had disappeared.

Naveen found himself standing on top of a cliff. Bhushan lay motionless way down at the bottom. The surface of this rocky cliff was very smooth and there was accumulated snow below. Naveen shivered with apprehension. He felt hopeless, desperate and lonely. "Bhushan, Bhushan," he shouted. But there was no reply. He mentally measured the depth of the cliff and concluded the drop to be thirty feet or more. Looking around, he could see no way of going down. He again shouted to Bhushan and to his relief there was some movement.

Gradually Bhushan regained his senses and got up. Even from a distance Naveen could see that there were blood smears on his forehead and his clothes were torn.

"Are you all right?" shouted Naveen.

"I think so," replied Bhushan weakly. "Perhaps the snow on the ground saved me." He looked around and said, "There seems to be no way of coming up."

Bhushan had some experience of rock climbing and tried to find hand-holds and foot-holds. He succeeded in climbing a few feet, but finding no further holds, had to jump back. He made many efforts to climb up while Naveen looked on helplessly. Then Naveen asked him to remain below while he sought help.

"No, you can't go alone, you will lose your way," shouted Bhushan. Naveen knew that he was right he would not be able to go alone nor could he help him in any other way except by letting him feel that he was not alone.

But Bhushan had not lost heart. He tried again, and found small foot-holds and hand-holds. He climbed slowly, clinging to the rock like a lizard; and at last, after two hours of labour, he was able to climb up.

Drops of perspiration shone on his forehead and blood oozed from his finger tips. But he was happy and felt exalted, relieved to be alive, having done something which he never had done before. Naveen gave him hot coffee from the thermos flask and some biscuits to eat.

However, they had not yet fulfilled the task for which they had set forth and it was already five o'clock. Realising that the others would be worried, they started to hurry back. They felt disappointed and their morale was low. Half-way down they heard the sound of bells coming from some distance—the sweetest sounds they had heard in there lives. The bells sounded closer, and soon they saw a man descending from the opposite slope accompanied by two mules. He too saw them.

"Are you the ones who are going to cross the Thamsar Pass?" he asked when he came nearer.

"Yes, and are you the one who will be accompanying us?" Bhushan asked.

"Yes, if you like."

Happy and relieved, Bhushan and Naveen said a silent prayer.

David, Pawan and Uncle Manjit met them on the way. They had set out from the village to look for them. "So at last you have found him," said Uncle.

"No, he found us," replied Bhushan, and he related the whole story.

Uncle Manjit looked at the muleteer and tried to study him. He was an extremely tall and well-built man, which was unusual in this area. All the people they had seen in the valley were of medium height. He was in his early forties and wore a Rajput style moustache. He had high cheekbones, a dominating chin and his eyes were clear, there was an aura of courage and honesty about him. Uncle was impressed with him.

"We shall like to hire one of your mules to carry our load over the Thamsar Pass," Uncle said.

"That I know," he affirmed.

"And what will you charge?" Uncle enquired.

"Sir, you people are outsiders. I am not like those corrupt freebooters and I am not one of those who exploit the situation," he replied.

"Still we shall like to know," Bhushan said.

"I shall charge you the official rate; and that is Rs 120 per day."

"Rupees one-hundred-and-twenty only? And up to which place?" Uncle thought that perhaps like the others he too would accompany them only till the top of the pass.

"I shall let you know everything," he said. "It will take two days to cross the pass and a further two days to reach the motor-head."

"And how much did you say you are going to charge for the entire four days march?"

"I told you, one-hundred-and-twenty rupees a day. And in case there is some delay somewhere due to some unforeseen circumstance, then you may add Rs. 40 for each additional day."

"And you will leave us at the motor-head?" Uncle Manjit confirmed, a little surprised.

"I shall leave you at Bir, the motor-head. From there you can get a bus for Baijnath or Pathankot."

"And how much load will one mule carry?"

"Sixty kilos," was the reply.

After all the uncertainties and suspense of two days, it sounded unbelievably good. The muleteer told them a great deal about the area and about himself. He seemed to be a good talker and a cheerful, jovial fellow.

He told them that the route from Chamba to Bara Banghal, through which they had come, was a bad one. The village was inhabited by people from Kulu, Kangra and Chamba valleys. Due to the presence of timber contractors and many other outsiders, the nature of the people of the area had also changed considerably.

"Are you also from Kulu or Kangra?" Naveen asked.

"No, I am a Gaddi from Brahmaur," he replied proudly.

While they were passing through the village, they saw the headman watching them from the balcony of his house. There was anger and contempt in his eyes.

"Look at him," the Gaddi said. "This crafty man is probably thinking of some plan to frustrate your efforts."

"But what can he do now?" Uncle Manjit said carelessly.

"Mark my words; he is a devious man. I know him very well. He has done a lot of harm to me too and we bear many grudges towards each other," he warned them.

"And may we know your name?" asked Uncle Manjit as he was leaving.

"Dhumer Singh," he replied.

* * *

They did not have to wait for long. They had hardly returned 'home' when the headman's henchman came to them and said sarcastically, "I see that you are planning to leave for the Thamsar Pass."

"Yes, you have guessed right. Any objection?" Uncle Manjit said contemptuously.

"I have a message from our respected headman and from our revered *chela*: the pass is not yet officially open."

"What do you mean by 'not officially open'?" Uncle felt his anger rising. "I don't care what you have to say. We are leaving tomorrow."

The henchman gave a crafty smile and said, "There is a deity of this *jot*(pass) called Thamsar *Devta*. The first man who crosses the pass each season is supposed to make some offering to the *Devta*," he explained.

"Do you mean to say that we are the first people to cross the pass?" Manjit asked.

"Yes, sir, it happens that you are the first people," was the reply.

"And what if we do not make the offering?" David wanted to know.

"Then the *Devta* will be angry and he will get his *bali* (sacrifice) forcibly. One of you will die in the snow. It has happened in the past and will happen now. No one dare defy the Gods," he warned

Seething with anger, Uncle Manjit said, "And what are the offerings which the first man is supposed to make?"

"Three he-goats," the henchman said. "You shall have to sacrifice one goat before you leave this place; the second, at the base of the pass; and the third at the top."

"The other day your headman did not mention anything about it and he was ready to send one of his men with us," Uncle commented. "Or did he quote a rate that included the price of the sacrificial goats?"

They neither had the money to purchase three goats nor had any intention of doing so. Dhumer Singh was not present and the shopkeeper was too timid to say anything.

"All right, we shall think it over and let you know," Uncle Manjit dismissed him.

"But I have not finished yet. Our headman and our revered *chela* asked me to warn you that if you try to leave this village for the Thamsar *Jot* without performing the said sacrifices, you will be responsible for the consequences." There was menace in his words and eyes.

When Dhumer Singh arrived, they described the entire episode to him. He listened, spat on the ground contemptuously and said, "That wilful, unscrupulous fellow, he has no respect or courtesy even for an outsider. He is telling a lie though not an absolute one."

"What do you mean 'not an absolute lie'?" Bhushan queried.

"The truth is that this sacrifice is a must but only once in every seven years. This is only the third year since the last sacrifice was performed. And moreover, three men have already crossed over the pass from the other side. It is certain that the headman is bent upon making trouble."

"But what do you suspect?" asked Bhushan.

"With the help of the *chela*, who is also a sort of witch doctor, he wants to extort money from you," explained Dhumer Singh.

"And what will his reaction be if we do not oblige him?" Bhushan asked.

"He will then gather some villagers and try to prevent you from leaving the village," warned Dhumer Singh. "And tomorrow if you leave you may find them waiting at the bridge."

"Then what should we do? Is there no police, no other authorities?" enquired David.

"No, there are no such authorities," he replied.

"Then we shall force our way out in case they try to stop us," Bhushan said.

"That will complicate matters all the more. But there is a simple way out. We could leave this place in the middle of the night," he suggested.

"Yes, that seems practical. But we shall have to cross the bridge over the Ravi, and for that we have to pass through the other side of the village where the headman resides. It is possible that we may be seen," Bhushan said.

"Don't worry about that. There is another way." Dhumer Singh outlined his plan: "During the night the temperature falls down considerably and the snow ceases to melt. The water level of the river also decreases. I know a place downstream where the water is shallow during the night. I used to cross the river from there when the bridge was broken three years ago."

After some more discussion, they agreed that they would leave the village at 3.00 a.m. By the time news of their departure reached the headman they would be many miles away and out of his reach.

It also meant that it was not possible to sleep that night.

They started packing immediately while the kind lady of the house cooked for them. As they were packing, Uncle Manjit asked each of them to carry their own sleeping bags, thermos flasks, waterbottles and a day's emergency ration with them in their rucksacks.

"But Uncle, why should we carry the load on our back now when the mule can carry everything?" Pawan protested.

"So that in case any of us gets lost he should be able to survive for at least twenty-four hours," Uncle explained.

"Do you anticipate such a thing, Uncle?" Naveen asked.

"I have heard of and experienced worse things in the mountains. One cannot imagine or foresee everything," Uncle cautioned. And Dhumer Singh nodded in agreement.

They purchased fresh provisions; thanked the kind shopkeeper who had given them shelter for two days; and gifted him their surplus sugar, milkpowder and other things. It was half-past three when they stood ready to leave, with the mule packed and loaded. They looked above. There was a half moon and the stars were shining in the sky. Bidding goodbye to the shopkeeper and his wife they left silently. Since this house was situated at the other end of the village, no one saw them leaving.

* * *

Soon they arrived at the riverbank. The water was shallow but freezingly cold. Luckily, they had a second mule which was walking without any load. They crossed the river on the back of that mule one by one.

After the two days' rest, their limbs were free of fatigue and they walked briskly. Walking under the shadow of the stars, in the dim silvery light of the half moon—the whole experience was something dream-like and different, and they felt exhilarated. The ascent was not very steep and they made good progress.

It was their first experience of trekking at night. Pawan and Naveen could not imagine that fading of night and coming of dawn could be so beautiful. The boys saw the stars disappearing one by one; the mass of light emerging from the east; and the mountains, the valley and the trees taking shape as if defined by the magic brush of an unseen painter.

THE MULETEER–DHUMER SINGH

When they felt that they were sufficiently away from the village, they stopped for a while to rest under a big tree. Soon they started talking to one another. Uncle asked Dhumer Singh, "What does Dhumer mean?"

"My father was a shepherd and I was born under the shadow of the Dhumer Mountain Range. So I was named Dhumer Singh," he replied .

"And what do you do? Don't you have any sheep?" Pawan asked.

"My father was left with only fifty sheep. Most of the herd were buried under an avalanche. It was difficult to make both ends meet. So when I grew up, I started working as a guide to survey parties.

"Once a group of foreigners came to our village. They wanted to climb some peaks and they engaged me as a guide. I know every inch of these mountains. At that time, I happened to save the life of an *Angrez* (Englishman). In return, he rewarded me handsomely, which enabled me to purchase three mules. Since then, I have been working as a muleteer."

* * *

The trekkers were on their feet again and soon found themselves on a narrow path along the Thamsar *Nala*. Due to the warmth of the sun, the snow on the mountain tops had begun to melt. The water in the stream flowed down with speed, thundering and winding its way through boulders and rocks.

"We have to reach the other side of the *nala*," Dhumer Singh said.

"Are we supposed to ford it?" Pawan asked.

"There is a small log bridge about one kilometre up. We shall cross it from there," replied Dhumer Singh.

Soon they came to the bridge—a flimsy looking one. The mules walked in the front. As they came close to the bridge, they sniffed and stopped. Dhumer Singh hit them lightly on the back, but they simply refused to budge.

"Your mules are afraid," Naveen said. Tiger too sniffed the ground uneasily.

Dhumer Singh said defensively, "These dumb animals are not cowardly. They are very clever. They have a sixth sense. Maybe there is something wrong with the bridge."

He checked the bridge and soon discovered a crack in one of the logs. He picked up a heavy rock, the size of a man's head, and threw it on the bridge, which could not withstand the impact. One side of it crumbled into the gushing waters and disappeared. They all shuddered at the thought of the disaster they had just escaped.

"Thank God we did not try to cross it," David sighed.

"Now what will we do?" Uncle Manjit asked.

"Don't worry, I will do something," Dhumer Singh assured them.

"But we should act quickly; otherwise the headman may catch up with us," Naveen said.

"Don't worry. If that rascal comes here, I will throw him into the stream. The Thamsar *Devta* will be only too happy to get his *bali*," he said, half jokingly and half seriously. But Pawan and Naveen were very happy to hear his words. They only wished that the headman would come and they could see the fight and ultimately see him disappearing into the cold water of the Thamsar stream.

Dhumer Singh picked up his big axe and disappeared into the nearby forest. Meanwhile, they took out their stove to prepare some tea.

Half an hour later Dhumer Singh returned. He was balancing a big log on his shoulder. Like a circus showman, he crossed the stream over what remained of the log bridge and asked Uncle Manjit to hold out one end of the log to him. Uncle followed his instructions and Dhumer Singh positioned the log over the stream at the right place. It took him another hour to fix and tie the planks to the log. Then they all crossed the bridge, step by step, their hearts in their mouths.

After all of them had crossed over, Dhumer Singh removed the log from the bridge in order to prevent the headman and his party crossing over. Pawan and Naveen were delighted by this move and decided that Dhumer Singh was an ace of a fellow to have with them.

Night in a Cave

When they were waiting on the bank of the stream, Naveen had removed his shoes and washed his feet in the stream. While walking barefoot on the rocks, he hurt one of his toes. Now, as he started climbing, his toe hurt so much that he was unable to keep pace with the others. David too was feeling very tired and both of them lagged behind the rest of the party. The gap between them and the others widened.

The weather, which in this area had always been unpredictable, started changing. Soon the whole sky was overcast. As Naveen and David gained height, the clouds also came closer and closer. Strong winds began to blow and the whole sky was filled with grey mist. The duo tried to quicken their pace but could not. After every attempt, they had to stop to catch their breath, and hoped to find their companions waiting for them at some turning point. But they found no one. They were annoyed and unhappy, imagining that no one cared to wait for them. They were overcome by the uneasy feeling that they had probably lost their way.

Suddenly they stopped. They had reached a dead end and found themselves standing on top of a gorge. Looking down, they could see the thin line of the stream at the bottom. Now they were certain that they had missed the track. Daylight had decreased to a strange greyish dimness and they felt imprisoned by the clouds.

Naveen and David stood there, lost, not knowing what to do or where to go. They searched for some sign of a track, but in vain. David called out loudly to their co-trekkers, but his voice seemed to lose itself in the grey mist without any response. The only other sound they could hear was that of the avalanches, which thundered down the slopes at short intervals.

The wind turned cold and chilly. They staggered and stumbled and the wind beat against them. Naveen shivered and clutched David's hand tight. He felt very lonely and frightened. His voice was choked with an unknown fear. He thought of his father and mother and longed to be in the warmth of his bed, secure in his home.

David read the fear on his face. He pressed Naveen's hand and said, "Don't worry, we shall find some shelter. When I was once trekking in the Canadian Rockies, something similar happened." And he started narrating his experience, partly to divert Naveen's attention and partly to help him gain courage and self-confidence. He looked around and led him to a hollow where several big boulders and a rock wall had made a sort of shallow cave. They entered the cave. Inside, in the semi-darkness, a strange smell filled the atmosphere. David took out his torch and shone it around. The cave was littered with brown hair. There were other signs too. It seemed that they were standing in the cave of a brown bear or some other wild animal.

David did not want to scare Naveen. He preferred to keep silent about his observation and said, "I don't think this is a good shelter. Let's go and find a better one."

"I do not have the energy," Naveen pleaded, "and this is good enough for a night's stay. I just want to lie down and sleep."

"Well, you wait here. I shall go out and look for another shelter," saying this, David went out. He searched for sometime, but in vain. He was afraid to stay away from Naveen for long, lest the bear came back.

There was no other alternative than to spend the night in the bear's cave. On his way to the cave, David collected dry wood. He was relieved to see that Naveen was safe and sound. 'Perhaps the bear will not come; perhaps it has abandoned this cave,' he thought to himself.

But still he did not want to take any risk. The first precaution to take was to make a fire and then to keep it burning the whole night. The wood was damp and it took him a long time to start the fire. He heaved a sigh of relief when the wood started burning, and collected more wood before darkness descended.

Then David cleared the ground, spread a waterproof sheet and the sleeping bags over it. Naveen immediately got into the sleeping bag. David poured him some hot coffee and opened a packet of biscuits. He drank the hot coffee and felt the warmth returning to his limbs. He looked at David with a grateful smile. David smiled back. In that short moment, sharing hardships and danger, they had become close friends.

Naveen cuddled inside the sleeping bag and was soon fast asleep. David was left awake, alone, in this strange unknown land, many thousand miles away from his homeland; alone, with the knowledge of a bear lurking outside. In his mind he thanked Uncle Manjit, who had advised them to keep one day's ration and the sleeping bags in their rucksacks. He himself felt dead tired. But he could not afford to sleep for he had to keep the fire burning the whole night. The fire made the cave warm and cozy. He wrapped himself with the sleeping bag, lighted a candle, took out a large knife and waited for the bear to make an appearance.

A certain numbness, born out of fear and the cold, pervaded his whole being. He had strange visions. He thought of his adventures in the mountains in Canadian Alaska and saw a Red-Indian or an Eskimo talking to him. Sometimes he dozed off, only to shake himself awake again. Just before midnight David heard the sound of snapping twigs and the rustle of dry leaves. He sensed a pair of eyes staring at him. He became alert at once. Throwing some more wood into the fire, he picked up the knife with one hand and switched on the torch with the other. He felt his heart thumping like a bellow. As the torch flashed, he saw two eyes glowing like red hot embers. His hair stood on end and a shiver ran down his spine. Suddenly a big dark object leaped backwards and disappeared behind the rocks. David heaved a sigh of relief and relaxed.

When Naveen opened his eyes the next morning, he saw David dozing with his head resting on his knees. He still held the knife in his hand. Naveen looked outside. The sky was clear and he could see the grass and rocks bathed in the morning light.

"Get up David Uncle, the night has passed," Naveen said touching his shoulder. David got up with a start. He looked around and as he recalled the night's episode, a mysterious smile touched his lips. The embers of fire, the wild animal lurking outside, the chilling experience, it all seemed like a dream. He wanted to keep it a secret, but at the same time could not hold it back from Naveen.

"Can you imagine, Naveen, that we have spent the night in a bear's cave," he said.

Naveen looked around and jumped up, "What! a bear's cave? How do you know?"

David told him everything. Naveen listened with awe and enquired, "Why did you not wake me up? I too would have liked to see a wild bear."

"Well, I shall wake you up the next time," David replied smiling.

They came out, washed themselves in a nearby stream, ate some biscuits, put on their shoes and climbed to the top of a ridge. They looked around and called out loudly to Uncle Manjit and the others. A little later, they heard Tiger's bark and then Uncle Manjit's voice, "Are you safe? Where are you . . . ?"

"We are here on the ridge above, to your left . . ." Naveen called back.

Tiger emerged from the boulders followed by Uncle Manjit and Dhumer Singh. They were happy to meet each other and narrated their experiences. What had happened the previous day was that at a certain point, instead of turning to the right, David and Naveen had kept on climbing straight, unmindful of the others, busy talking to each other. The had walked along a dried water course, which had somehow looked like a beaten track; it had taken them away from the main party.

* * *

Now that the group had reunited they continued with their trek. Their next campsite was situated amidst snow-covered peaks. It was an ideal site for camping. There was a big sheet of ice nearby and water trickled beneath it, appearing and disappearing, playing hide-and-seek with the ice.

As the tents were being pitched in the pastureland, David gathered wild spinach from the slopes, and Dhumer Singh unharnessed the mules, which started grazing on the soft grass. A Gaddi shepherd who was already there with his flock of sheep, joined Dhumer Singh. They collected dry wood and lit a fire between some boulders.

Slowly the sun sank behind the mountains, casting long shadows on the slopes. The cliffs that had looked bluish-grey during day-time, now turned black. The white snow-covered peaks and the shining glacier posed a great contrast. On top of a cliff stood two wild goats looking down at the tents curiously.

The night was cold and frosty. The trekking party went inside the tents, while the two Gaddis squatted on the blanket spread out near the fire. After some time, the two of them leaned against the big rock that loomed behind them and snuggled inside their blankets. Occasionally during the night, one of them would open his eyes, throw a piece of wood in the fire, and go back to sleep.

Climbing the Pass

Dhumer Singh told them that the ascent to Thamsar Pass would be long and strenuous. It was also necessary that they cross it before noon, because in the afternoon strong winds and blizzards begin to blow, and this could give rise to dangerous situations.

After an early breakfast, they filled their flasks with hot coffee and were on the move before the sun rose. The small party crossed a green meadow, walked over a sea of stones and boulders and trekked over the moraine—a vast collection of rock and gravel, formed by the glacier—till they reached the glacier itself. Due to the extreme cold, the snow beneath their feet was hard and slippery like a sheet of glass. They made slow progress slipping, stumbling at an altitude of about 13,000 feet, where the thin air made breathing difficult.

On both sides of the glacier there were rocky mountains, like two parallel walls. After some time, the rock walls disappeared and in their place appeared shining white snow slopes.

In the morning, Pawan and Naveen had been looking forward to walking on the snow. From a distance it had looked so beautiful and beckoning. But at close

quarters the snow was harsh and unfriendly. As they walked on, their hands and noses started freezing. There was nothing but the long walk on the white snow, the terrible silence and the freezing cold. Soon they felt tired.

They sat down on a single rock thrusting out of the snow.

"I did not know that walking on snow could be so torturous," said Pawan, staring at the open endless expanse of snow as he rubbed his palms to warm up.

"This is nothing, young master," Dhumer Singh said. "Climb the pass and you will be in the warmth of the sun again." He continued, "It is only when you have to walk in the snow day after day with no tree, no grass, no gurgling stream; to walk in ankle-deep snow, with only snow to eat, snow to sit on and snow to sleep on, that you come close to madness. I have known it; it happened to me once," Dhumer Singh said with a distant look in his eyes. His voice sank to a whisper as if he was reliving some horrifying experience.

Naveen no longer stared at the snowy wilderness. Dhumer Singh's talk made him curious, and he asked him to tell him more.

"I will tell you," said Dhumer Singh. "It was long ago when I was young, hot-blooded and foolish. We were three people with five mules and a dog. Our mules were loaded with wheat, rice and other things. We were coming from Manali towards Bara Banghal through the treacherous Kaliheni Pass. It was not the month of June but of April. The winter snow had not yet melted and it was all snow, nothing but snow, from beginning to end.

"For three days we walked in the snow, sleeping at night in the caves in the mountainside which we knew very well. The weather had been bad all through and we had not seen the sun for two days. It was so cold that the moisture of our breathing settled on our moustaches."

"I was leading the mules, who were moving reluctantly, and my dog trotted besides me. It was a big sheepdog with a thick hairy coat, almost the size of a bear. I had fixed a nailed collar around his neck and he had successfully fought many snow leopards and bears. After days of continuous travel on the snow, the animals too looked depressed and miserable. But the worst was yet to come. Before the sun set we were faced with a terrible blizzard.

"The powdery snow hit our faces and we could see nothing except whiteness all around. The snow became softer and deeper. We started sinking in the snow. One by one our mules sank and died. We could not save them for we knew that as long as we were able to walk we could pump the blood in our veins. If we stopped, our blood circulation would stop.

"It became completely dark, while the blizzard continued. We could not walk in the darkness. Luckily, we saw a few boulders thrusting upwards from the snow. We recognized that landmark and were able to find a shelter beneath the boulders.

"We all sat down and wrapped ourselves in blankets. My dog sat huddled against me for warmth. I covered him also with my blanket. But soon we discovered that it was no better. It was extremely cold. I knew that first the toes of the feet would freeze and then the fingers of the hand would become numb and then the whole body . . . . And I saw this happening to my two companions. Their heads fell on their knees as if they had fallen asleep. I wanted to say; 'Don't sleep, get up and warm your hands and feet; don't let yourselves be frozen to death.' But I could not wake them. I myself was feeling very weak and miserable.

I did not want to die. 'I must do something,' I told myself. I remembered the stories told by my grandfather. I picked up my axe and with great effort pressed it on my finger with all the weight of my body. I did not feel the pain as my finger cut into two. I saw the blood oozing through the open wound. I sipped my blood slowly. Due to the oozing of the blood there was a continuous flow of blood in my veins. It was a long and frightful night. I had nightmares and saw the spirits of many people who had died in the snows in the past.

"With the first rays of the sun I realised that I was alive. The warmth of the dog who had been lying in my lap also helped me to keep myself warm. I touched my companions. They were dead and cold, like stone."

Dhumer Singh stopped talking. His mouth had dried up. He took a mouthful of snow and started sucking it.

Pawan and Naveen looked at him with wonder and admiration, and also looked at his missing finger, which they had not noticed earlier.

"And I tell you, my little sirs," he continued, "while on the move don't drink water too often or too much, otherwise you will have cramps in your stomach. Never get impatient with the mountains; climb slowly and steadily, keeping rhythm with your breath and do not stop for rest too frequently . . . ." He gave them a broad smile and it seemed that he had enjoyed narrating this story. "And now let us walk on," he said. "We still have a long way to go."

They started climbing again, slowly. Their hearts raced; their steps faltered. The pass was visible, but still very far away. The snow creates illusions—illusions of perception—so that distances look shorter than they really are.

It was ten o'clock and the rays of the sun were falling directly on the snow. They wore dark glasses to protect their eyes. The heat of the sun was reflected by the snow. The felt hot inside their heavy clothes.

"You do not know how quickly the weather changes here," Manjit said. They were sweating and small streams of perspiration were running down their body. They felt thirsty and exhausted and prayed that either the pass be brought closer or that something happen so that they could be saved from the unbearable heat of the sun.

It seemed that God heard their prayer, because soon clouds appeared from behind the mountains. Slowly and silently the grey mist surrounded them from all sides. Pawan and Naveen felt happy and relieved. Soon the mist grew so thick that they could hardly see for more than a few feet.

"Which way to go?" If they took one wrong step, made one move in the wrong direction, they would miss the pass. It was so completely and utterly silent that they could hear their own heartbeats. The jingling of the bells around the mules' necks emphasized the surrounding silence.

But the muleteer knew the path well. Dhumer Singh had the courage and understanding of a true mountaineer. He was perfectly composed. His limbs moved instinctively; although somewhere at the back of his mind he carried the pictures of those fellow-travellers who had been buried in the snow and were never seen again.

"There are crevasses and hidden pools of water beneath the snow. So you must not wander. Just follow my footsteps closely," Dhumer Singh warned them.

"Once I was crossing this pass with my uncle," he began. "The weather turned bad. The snow was soft and deep. Men and mules sank in the ankle-deep snow. At certain points there were hidden pools of water beneath. Somehow or the other the mules crossed the bad patch. But my uncle was caught in it. He sank into the snow until he disappeared from sight altogether."

"And why did you not do anything?" Pawan asked.

"It all happened so suddenly that I was taken by surprise. I was walking a little distance behind and when I rushed to the spot to help, the snow had already swallowed him. There was not a trace of him in the soft snow, as if my uncle had never existed."

"You are exaggerating," Bhushan said.

"Whether you believe it or not, only two years ago, when there was less snow on the pass and the heavy rains had made the previous snow melt, some passersby saw him appear from under the snow. After ten years of being buried in the snow, it looked as if he had died just yesterday. Even his clothes and his leather purse were intact."

After sometime Dhumer Singh started leading his mules. He had tied one end of his white turban around his face, his eyes were covered with sunglasses. The bells around the mules necks jingled. Sometimes Dhumer Singh would stop on a snow ridge and look at the path. It seemed as if he was not a man from this age and time, but someone who had emerged from the distant past, and a superman, like a warrior or a pioneer. Maybe he had been a leader in his previous birth, when his Aryan ancestors crossed these mountain frontiers two or three thousand years ago.

And then it started snowing. Pawan and Naveen stopped to watch the cotton-like snow falling from the sky. They were excited and Naveen stretched out his hand to feel it. All around there was absolutely nothing but the falling flakes of white snow, falling silently on their shoulders, their rucksacks, and their clothes.

It had been snowing in the upper parts of the mountains for the last three days. Therefore, the snow had not yet settled. The fresh snow made matters worse. The trekkers, along with their mules, were being thrust into the ankle-deep snow. Walking became difficult. The powdery snow found its way through the socks into their shoes, making their feet damp and socks soggy. At many places, due to their heavy loads, the mules sank into the snow up to their thighs. They had to be pulled out. Everyone was reminded of the horrible story which Dhumer Singh had narrated, but no one dared to speak about it.

Journeying ahead they came across a deep, blue glacial lake amidst the snow. They had to negotiate a steep slope which ended in the lake. Sometimes a heap of snow would be dislocated by the impact of their footsteps and would start rolling down, accumulating and carrying more and more snow with it, finally falling with a thud into the silent cold water. It was beautiful, but they did not have the time or energy to appreciate it.

As they gained height, it became colder. The cold wind stung their faces and stabbed their ears. Their feet were icy cold and they wanted to remove their wet socks. But it was no use doing so, their feet would get wet again anyway.

"How far is the pass?" David asked.

"It is very near, but we are moving very slowly," Dhumer Singh answered.

"How much more time will it take to reach there?" Pawan queried.

"Maybe an hour," was the discouraging reply.

They plodded on and on, dragging their feet with great effort. They felt that the packs on their back were growing heavier and heavier. The weather had cleared a bit. In fact they had climbed beyond the clouds, above 16,500 feet, and could see the clouds floating below them. At last they saw another ridge against the skyline, with spires and peaks on its left and right.

"That is the Thamsar Pass," declared Dhumer Singh.

To reach the pass, they had to climb an almost perpendicular looking snow-wall. As they climbed, the powdery snow slipped and crumbled under their feet, making them slide down, again and again. They kicked the snow with their shoes and pulled themselves up with great effort. With desperate courage, unmindful of the pain in their ankles and feet, one by one they climbed to the top of the pass.

What a relief it was. The joy they felt was unlike anything they had ever experienced before. Pawan and Naveen felt their bodies tingle as they stepped onto the top of the pass. For the past so many days they had been walking, talking and thinking about this place. Now they stopped to look at the awe-inspiring panorama of the snow-covered peaks from the pass. They danced and embraced one another in excitement. They were happy that they had climbed up 16,500 feet high, something which no one in their class or even in their school had done. The thrill was something beyond words. They forgot the pain in their feet. They unloaded their rucksacks and sat down on the jumble of rocks.

Everyone removed their wet socks and dried their feet. Mercifully, the sun appeared. The warmth of the sun enwrapped them and they felt good. But David sat apart, silent. His toes had turned white and he was crying in pain. He was suffering from chilblain as the blood circulation had stopped in his toes.

Uncle Manjit lifted his pullover, held David's feet in his hand and made them touch his warm and dry belly. Bhushan took out his sleeping bag and wrapped it around David's legs. Slowly and steadily, the warmth returned to his feet and he felt great relief. A hot cup of coffee also proved very refreshing. Half an hour later, a smile mingled with tears appeared on his face. He said, "I am a stranger to you and to your land. You have done so much for me that I can never thank you enough."

"You were a stranger when we met first, but not now," Uncle Manjit said. "There is a saying that if you walk seven steps with a stranger, he becomes your friend, and if you spend seven nights with him he becomes your brother."

In the shadow of a high rock the Thamsar *Devta* resided. Dhumer Singh offered his prayers to the God and tied a piece of cloth to a *trishul*. Pawan and Naveen also did the same. Many small *trishuls* were placed beside the rock. Uncle Manjit, Bhushan and the others also offered prayers for a safe journey.

HOMEWARDS

Before leaving, Pawan and Naveen turned to take one last look at the region they had traversed. They could see the mountain ranges of Chamba and Brahmaur; some of the streams looked like streaks of silver. Beyond that they could also see the snow-covered peaks of the Pir Panjal Range, spreading 300 kilometres, from Kulu to Kashmir. It was a magnificent view, which only a mountaineer or a trekker could enjoy, for no picture or words can describe it adequately.

The descent was easy and difficult as well at times. As they put their feet on the loose powdery snow, it would slide one or two feet down. In that way they could cover more distance with each step. Quite often, they would lose their balance and fall. But since the snow was soft, it did not hurt. On one occasion when Naveen fell, he went sliding down for twenty metres or more. He found it very amusing and an easier way to cover the distance without using his legs. They covered the first few kilometres without much effort, sliding, glissading on the snow, and enjoyed it.

The descent to this side of Dhauladhar was steeper than the other side. The landscape was beautiful. There were high snow peaks on one side and bare rocky cliffs on the other. In between, was the glacier on which they were now walking. A few clouds played hide-and-seek with the snow-covered peaks. As the sun sank behind the mountains, it turned cold. The snow also became harder. The trekkers slipped and fell often. When they had to cover a steep stretch, they had to cut steps with the help of an ice axe.

Suddenly Naveen saw a long thin line on the glacier below. "What is that," he enquired.

"That seems to be a crevasse," Bhushan replied.

"A crevasse? You mean a crack in the snow?"

"Yes, a big deep crack. Due to the alternating heat of the sun during the day and the freezing cold at night, the ice expands and shrinks. Sometimes it cracks and these crevasses are formed," Bhushan explained.

"You just follow my footsteps," Dhumer Singh reminded them. "There are many such crevasses;

sometime you can see them, sometimes not, especially when they are hidden under the fresh snow. If you accidentally step on it, then down you go into the icy hole."

Pawan and Naveen shuddered at the thought of falling into a crevasse. Uncle Manjit thought it safer to tie a rope around everyone's waist so that if someone happened to fall into a crevasse, the others could hold the rope and save him from rolling down too far.

Thus they continued their descent. They crossed the stone-littered moraine, where the glacier ended and the stream began; forded many streams, and at last saw wisps of smoke rising from down below.

"That is Supdhar, our next halt," Dhumer Singh said.

The sun had already set. They could see a few buffaloes grazing in a grassy field far down. By this time they had climbed 4000 feet, descended almost the same height and had covered about 25 kilometres. They had been on their feet for thirteen hours. Their legs refused to move any further and their ankles ached. Pawan and Naveen had never before been through such an experience, which made so many demands on the body and mind.

When they reached the grassy meadow, they lay down exhausted. Dhumer Singh collected some wood, made a big fire and brought fresh milk from the Gujjars who lived nearby. It was a great pleasure to sit around the fire and drink fresh, hot milk.

They were too tired to unpack their rucksacks and pitch their tents. Luckily they found a big cave beside a stream. They spread their sleeping bags inside and crawled into them. When they were comfortably settled, Pawan and Naveen looked around carefully. It was spotlessly clean and some dry grass was spread on the ground. There was a hearth in one corner and the roof above was black with smoke.

Uncle Manjit told them that it was just possible that this cave was the home of people in the Stone Age. And perhaps the first Aryans who crossed these mountains many hundred years ago might have stayed in the same cave. This cave was now regularly used by passing shepherds and stray travellers who happened to pass on this route. They saw a small heap of dried wood piled up besides the makeshift hearth. According to the prevailing custom, whoever passed the night in these cave shelters used the firewood, and in the morning left fresh dry wood for later travellers who might stop by.

Pawan and Naveen were asleep immediately due to sheer exhaustion. They had strange dreams. They saw the Stone-Age hunters returning to the cave after a hunting expedition, barbecuing meat on a fire in front of the cave, with bears and snow leopards prowling all around.

The next morning they resumed their downward journey. They passed through a dense forest; lost their way twice, but found it again soon; passed through small villages and after crossing a stream wading through knee-deep water, at last reached the small town of Bir.

They sat down on wooden chairs in a small tea-shop and ordered tea. It was a luxury to sit on chairs instead of hard cold stones. The sweet shop, ready-made tea, even the water tap seemed to be a thing of luxury. Now they did not have to go to a stream to fetch water, or to boil snow on their stove.

Pawan and Naveen looked at the road and the bus. "What a relief to be able to just sit back and let the bus take you to your destination," Pawan said.

They looked upwards, towards the high snow-capped peaks. They could hardly believe that they had just crossed those awe-inspiring mountains.

"How could we do it?" Naveen said, his voice full of pride and achievement.

"Because," said Uncle Manjit quietly, "because each of us has got hidden reserves of energy within us."

Both the boys had developed a great liking for Dhumer Singh. They invited him to come to Delhi with them. But he politely declined saying, "Thank you sirs, but I belong to these mountains. This is my world and I have no desire to go elsewhere."

"Come again," Dhumer Singh said while parting, "and I will take you across the other passes in the heart of the mountains where no outsider has ever dared to set foot."

"We shall definitely come back to the mountains," they assured him.

* * *

When they reached Dalhousie, they invited David to dinner. Over the meal, they recounted their experiences of the trek and talked till midnight.

Pawan and Naveen introduced Tiger to their mother saying, "Next time when we go trekking, we will leave Tiger with you. He will keep you company." At this, Tiger growled as if to say, "No, I shall also go with you . . . ."